The Magic of Winter

Written by: Abby Slife · illustrated by: Danny Reneau

To learn more about David Romanelli, please visit: www.davidromanelli.com.

The heart of coffee and tea as universal human connectors is explored across nine countries in the feature documentary, *The Connected Cup*. To watch or learn more visit: www.theconnectedcup.com.

To learn more about Colorado Kids Academy, please visit: www.cokidsacademy.com.

ISBN 978-1-7331491-0-5 (hardcover)

Book designed by Abby Slife, Danny Reneau, Phil Whitmarsh and Ryan Simanek.

This book was hand lettered by Abby Slife.

Published by Blue Sky Dreamer, LLC.

Printed in the United States of America.

For my beloved family...
With all my heart, thank you.

♡ABBY

For my 3 boys, who are a
constant reminder of the good
 in this world.
And to my beautiful wife,
 who's love and support makes
me a better person.
— Danny

" Hey, Mom, come quick!
It's SNOWING!!! "

"May I go outside and play?"

"Of course, little one.
Let's get you dressed and
ready for fun!"

What a glorious gift
to wake up to
new fallen snow!

I dash down the stairs
as fast as I can.

I bundle up quickly in
my winter gear.
I'm ready to dive in!

I bolt out the door.
BRRRRR!!!

It's chilly out here.

But the sun is shining brightly
on my face, and I am
toasty warm.

I run!

I jump!

I dance!

It's my own winter wonderland!

I grab an icicle and create
magic in the snow.

It's amazing what I can make happen with my imagination!

The snow is perfect
for making snowballs
and snowmen.

I toss snowballs at anyone who dares to enter my domain.

Out of the blue, I stop.
I am feeling slightly cold.

I start to think of hot chocolate.

Dad makes it best. I hope he remembers the marshmallows. Yum... I can taste it already... warm and delicious!

But wait! Before I go inside,
I need to make a snow angel...
my favorite!

I fall back into a mountain
of fresh powder. It is so
soft and inviting.

I feel like I am in my
mom's warm cuddles.

I am nestled in the earth,
my arms swiftly moving up
and down, back and forth.

Suddenly, I'm not in
my yard anymore...

I am a playful king penguin swimming...

...in an Antarctic blue sea
of peace and joy.

Then, I transform into...

... a mighty polar bear. Exploring the tundra, I am majestic and strong.

I am the King of all I see!
My heart sings at the
sight of the beauty that
surrounds me.

As I move through the
frozen terrain, my arms
become wings, and now I am...

... gliding through the crystal-clear sky like a northern cardinal.

I am full of grace.
My red feathers are
stunning against the
stark-white snow.

Ahhhhh... I am free in the snow.
In the comforting embrace of
my snow angel, I can be
anything I want to be.

I think I'll stay here just a little bit longer.
This is the magic of winter.

" Everything you can imagine is real."

– Pablo Picasso

Winter Bucket List

Please partner with your family to enjoy some of these fun-filled activities this winter!

- ☐ Make homemade snow cones or ice cream from fresh snow!
- ☐ Pick a winter-inspired book to read as a family, while snuggling.
- ☐ Explore your yard for animal and/or bird tracks.
- ☐ Create a family vision board for the New Year – Dream big!
- ☐ Enjoy a winter camp out in your living room and make s'mores in the microwave.
- ☐ Give someone an unexpected, homemade gift (bonus if it's winter-themed).
- ☐ Make sock puppets and perform a puppet show.
- ☐ Watch your favorite holiday movie at home with treats.
- ☐ Gather old towels and blankets to donate to your local animal or homeless shelter.
- ☐ Decorate cookies and share with someone special and sweet.
- ☐ Feed winter birds by building a pinecone birdfeeder.
- ☐ Learn how to make hot cocoa from scratch.
- ☐ Help shovel a neighbor's sidewalk and/or driveway.
- ☐ Visit a museum in your town/city (see if they offer a kid-friendly, scavenger hunt).
- ☐ Build your own yummy, gooey pizza for dinner.
- ☐ Perform random acts of kindness throughout the season.
- ☐ Catch snowflakes on your tongue.
- ☐ Look at snowflakes under a magnifying glass and then make paper snowflakes based on what you see.
- ☐ Enjoy a cozy pajama day ALL DAY!
- ☐ Create a gratitude list and add to it regularly.
- ☐ Write and illustrate a "sequel" to a book you love.
- ☐ Send a card/postcard to someone who inspires you and tell them why.

- ☐ Collect toys, books, and clothes that you no longer need and donate locally.
- ☐ Build your own snow globe with lots of glitter!
- ☐ Pretend it is summer and indulge in an indoor picnic.
- ☐ Three words: Board Game Day!
- ☐ Read by the fireplace or with a flashlight under your covers.
- ☐ Enjoy an indoor snowball fight with cotton balls, yarn balls, or loofahs.
- ☐ Create a fun winter playlist for a family dance party!
- ☐ Funny family photo shoot with hats, scarves, and mittens.
- ☐ Go sledding on a sunny day!
- ☐ Work on a ginormous jigsaw puzzle.
- ☐ Bundle up in as much outdoor wear possible and then compete in a penguin race around your backyard. Challenge your neighbors to a friendly penguin race!

ABBY Slife debuts as a children's author with The Magic of Winter. It is the first in a series of four books, that encourage outdoor play, combined with imagination and celebration of the season.

Abby fosters her love of reading in Ankeny, Iowa with her jack-of-all-trades husband, her two benevolent sons, and her four-legged friends through gardening, supporting teachers and students as a Special Education Paraeducator, hospice volunteering, and exuding joy wherever the wind takes her!

Follow Abby on Instagram ... @abbylslife

Danny Reneau of Lincoln, Nebraska, began drawing in the fourth grade. Inspired by other artists, music, nature and his family, Danny sketches each illustration in pencil and then brings his work to life with watercolor and ink.

In addition to painting, Danny enjoys going on walks through local nature reserves with his family, discovering great local art, and introducing his three young boys to 90's rock and roll whether they are in the mood for it or not.

Follow Danny on Instagram ... @danny.reneau